Caz Robinson

Dylan's Nursery Adventures:

The Playground Jungle

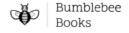

Bumblebee
Books

A CIP catalogue record for this
title is available from the British
Library.

ISBN: 978-1-83934-677-4

Bumblebee Books is an imprint of
Olympia Publishers.

First Published in 2023

Bumblebee Books Tallis
House
2 Tallis Street London
EC4Y 0AB

Printed in Great Britain

Dedication

I dedicate this book to our gorgeous son Dylan
and his beautiful sister, Leah.

Dylan always looked forward to nursery days.

He always had such exciting adventures
with his friends!

Although Dylan hated seeing how sad his mum
was to leave him to go to work, he knew that
if he hugged her really tightly before she left,
then she would be ok.

Once his mum had left and he had
his breakfast, Dylan began looking around
for clues about today's adventure.

"Ball?" he asked Michelle hopefully,
picking up his favourite toy.

"Not today, Dylan", she replied patiently.

"Animals?" asked Liam, joining his partner in crime at his side.

The boys were looking up at the box of animals stacked at the side of the room.

"Maybe later…" replied Sarah as she walked over to join the group.

"Hmmmmmm…" the boys looked
around for more ideas.

"Drawing?" Dylan asked, looking up at some of the colourful masterpieces on the wall of the nursery.

Michelle paused, just long enough to get the attention of all of her little explorers.

"You're going to need your shoes on children, we're going outside this morning!"

"Yay!" they all chorused and ran to get their shoes.

Michelle and Sarah helped the children down the stairs and outside.

"Are you ready for today's adventure?" asked Sarah.

"Yeahhhhh!" the children squealed.

Sarah and Michelle helped the children onto the aeroplane, ready to fly off for their newest adventure.

They travelled round and around, far, far away, deep into the jungle.

When they landed, the children jumped into the jeeps and raced each other along the dirt roads to the centre of the jungle.

They wandered through the jungle
trees and grass...

… and rummaged in the foliage, searching for jungle critters to look at and safe berries to snack on.

Dylan and his friends then prowled through the jungle floor on their hands and knees, like big cats, hunting for their prey.

They climbed over rocks,
and under branches.

They climbed onto the back of an elephant, and slid down his trunk, all the way down to the floor!

Dylan led his friends flying like birds,
soaring through the sky...
... gliding through the jungle, playfully.

Next, Dylan, Liam and their friends slithered
like snakes across the jungle floor and raced
each other like leaping frogs.

They swung through the trees like the monkeys do. The views from the top were amazing!

Then they dug for treasure to
take home to Mum!

And then, treasure in hand,
they made it safely home…

...just in time for lunch!!

About the Author

As a teacher of PE for 15 years, I had been looking for new challenges to motivate and inspire me. When I became a mum I loved the idea of writing about my own children and the adventures that we would have. As a first time writer on maternity leave, I loved hearing about my son's adventures and games at nursery, so I tried to capture some of our memories, which will become a memento for us forever.

Acknowledgements

Thank you to my husband Dean for encouraging me, and our children, Dylan and Leah, for inspiring me.